Copyright © 2020 Claire E. Hallinan

All rights reserved. No part of this publication may be reproduced, distributed, or transmitted in any form or by any means, including photocopying, recording, or other electronic or mechanical methods, without the prior written permission of the publisher, except in the case of brief quotations embodied in reviews and certain other non-commercial uses permitted by copyright law.

ISBN 978-1-7330356-6-8

Where My Breath ♥ Loves Me

Written by
Claire E. Hallinan

Illustrated by
Charity Russell

To Mrs. Hallinan 's Champions in
2019 - 2020

The breath is a gift given when we are born.

Mr. Gentleheart is a guest teacher. Twice a week he visits our class to teach something unique called mindfulness. Mr. Gentleheart tells us, "Mindfulness is a tool for peace in our lives." In his lessons, Mr. Gentleheart has taught us different breathing techniques like Belly Breathing, Counting Breaths, and Tracing Finger Breathing.

My favorite practice is the Alligator Breath. I take a deep breath while stretching my arms out and opening them like an alligator's mouth. Then I slowly breathe out as my alligator mouth closes. With only one alligator breath, my energy level goes down and I feel settled.

At the end of the lesson, Mr. Gentleheart invites us to put our hands on our hearts. Then, he taps his singing bowl with a little wooden hammer. The rich, deep sound echoes through the classroom and sinks deep into my heart.

I open my eyes and notice that Mr. Gentleheart is hugging himself really tight. Sometimes I wonder whether Mr. Gentleheart is being funny or serious. I hear him whisper,
"Oh, I love my breath. And my breath loves me!" Then, he pauses.
Mr. Gentleheart announces, "In the next lesson, please be ready to share where you feel the love from your breath."

Love? From my breath? I am confused. I feel calm when I practice breathing, but I never thought of my breath loving me.

"Hey, breaths, do you love me?" I listen to my breaths for a few moments, but I don't hear a thing.

Where do I have to go to find the answer?

Does my breath love me?

I am curious and eager to discover the place where my breath loves me.

In music class, Mrs. Treble leads the voice warm-up. "Keep your shoulders still, and just breathe in through your stomach. Great! Then, breathe out with a 'v' sound, vvvvvv... Do you feel your belly falling in flat? Belly breathing is important to help control the volume and quality of your voice," Mrs. Treble explains.

Each time Mrs. Treble gives us a new note, we breathe with our bellies rising up and falling down. It is just like Mr. Gentleheart's Belly Breathing exercise. Soon, the "v" sound becomes regular lyrics and we start
to sing a song.

Keeping up with the belly breathing and singing makes
me feel joyous, as if my breath is coaching me. Is the
choir room the place where my breath loves me?

Our classroom teacher, Mr. Pi, is Mr. Gentleheart's best friend. That is why we have a special guest teacher anyway. Although Mr. Pi is one of the nicest teachers, today's math is so confusing. As soon as we start our worksheet, Mr. Pi walks through the rows of desks. My heart starts racing as his footsteps approach my desk.

Mr. Pi eyes my scribbles and softly whispers in my ear, "I see you are struggling. Take a big breath. It might take some time, but struggles make your brain stronger." And he circles a part of the numbers that I scratched on my paper and then leaves like the wind. Breathe in, breathe out, it might take some time... and boom!

Suddenly, my mind lights up like a light bulb as if my breath connected the circled numbers with my brain. My pencil moves crazily over my worksheet until it completes the problem.

I take another big breath, smile, and put my pencil down. I whisper to myself, "I did it!" I feel satisfied. My heart is no longer racing, as if my breaths rescued me from my math agony.

Is the classroom the place where my breath loves me?

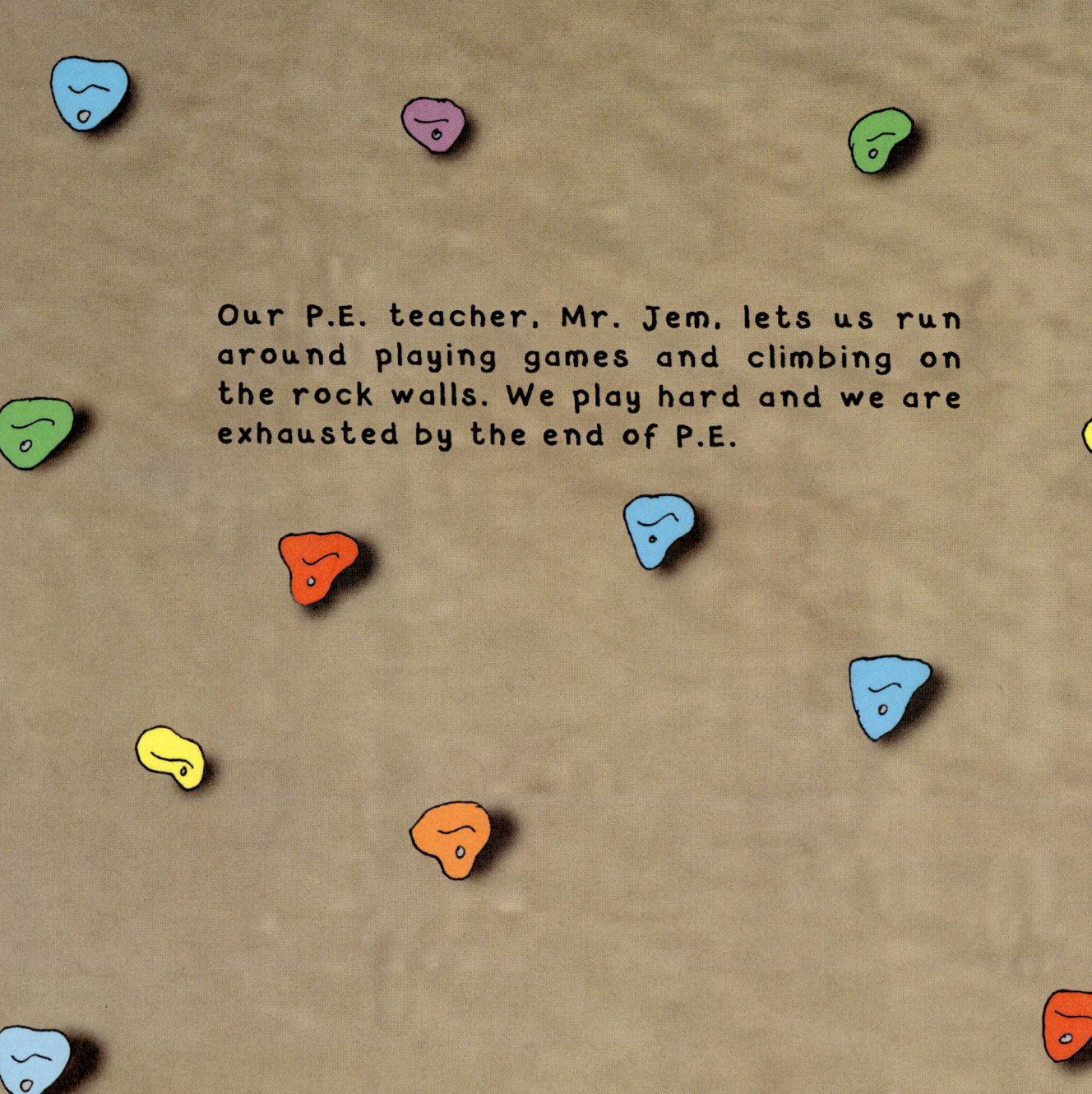

Our P.E. teacher, Mr. Jem, lets us run around playing games and climbing on the rock walls. We play hard and we are exhausted by the end of P.E.

Mr. Jem says, "Okay, guys, let's take a big, deep breath. Your heart is going to relax little by little. Notice the change of your breaths. Your breaths are getting close to your resting rhythm.
Be curious about how they become your normal breaths.

Before my third big breath, my whole body quiets down with pleasantness. I feel peaceful, as if my breaths soothe me.

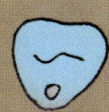

Is the gym the place where my breath loves me?

We often read books independently when we are with Mr. Reed in the library. Sometimes he suggests using reading strategies, like visualization.

Mr. Reed says, "Before you turn a page, pause and breathe. When you close your eyes, you can see the movie scene that you have just read. The better understanding of what the author wants you to take away from the book, the more vivid your movie becomes."

I feel excited to see the movie in my head, as if my breath creates a cinema screen.

Is the library the place where my breath loves me?

Mr. Woods, the science teacher, takes us outside. Each of us has a hand lens to observe fallen leaves on the ground.

Mr. Woods says, "Everybody, take a big breath. You can observe delicate lines and different colors on the leaves. All of the
important nutrients and water seep through these thin tubes so they can survive, just like your blood vessels. Isn't it amazing to learn how a plant's life lines are just like a human's?"

To be honest, art is not my favorite, especially painting. My painting always looks messy, not artsy. But I like Ms. Da Vinci, our art docent. Ms. Da Vinci tells us, "Breathe. Own your mistakes. Your mistakes will no longer be mistakes when you own them."

In fact, an accidental red drop merges with green and brown on my construction paper. The leaf I am coloring becomes more realistic, like the first sign of autumn.

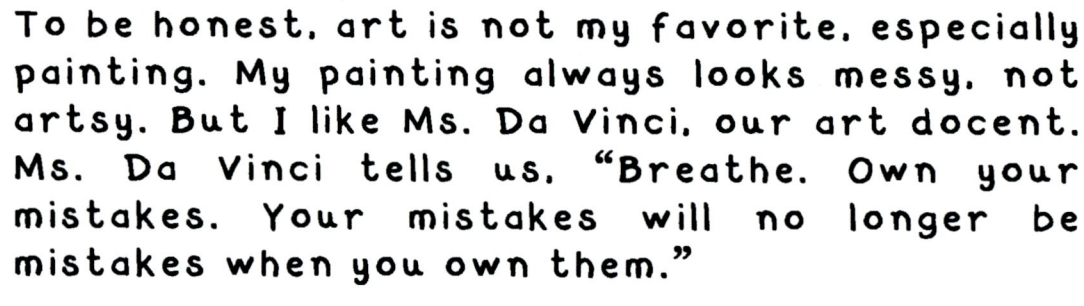

After school, my mother takes me to my swimming lesson. Our coach, Ms. Finn, tells us, "We are going to float a little longer than the last time with a cool breathing technique. Breathe in through your mouth and out with your nose, like this." She sucks up the air through her mouth, then submerges her face into the water and blows bubbles through her nose. "Now it's your turn."

Usually, I am good at breathing in through my nose and out through my mouth, but this is the total opposite. Curiously, I breathe in through my mouth and dunk my face into the water. As I blow the air out through my nose, it is kind of ticklish.

I enjoy the sensation in my nose and continue to practice as if my breath plays a game with me.

Is the swimming pool the place where my breath loves me?

At the coffee shop, my mom treats me with a cup of hot cocoa, just because of how brave I was in swimming class. She tells me, "Smell your hot cocoa and blow it to cool it down."

My heart melts with the sweetened chocolate sensation traveling into my nose and onto my taste buds.

I love my breath for bringing me such a joyous body sensation. I feel full of gratitude for my breath that transforms my life experiences into calmness, curiosity, and happiness.

Does this mean my breath loves me?

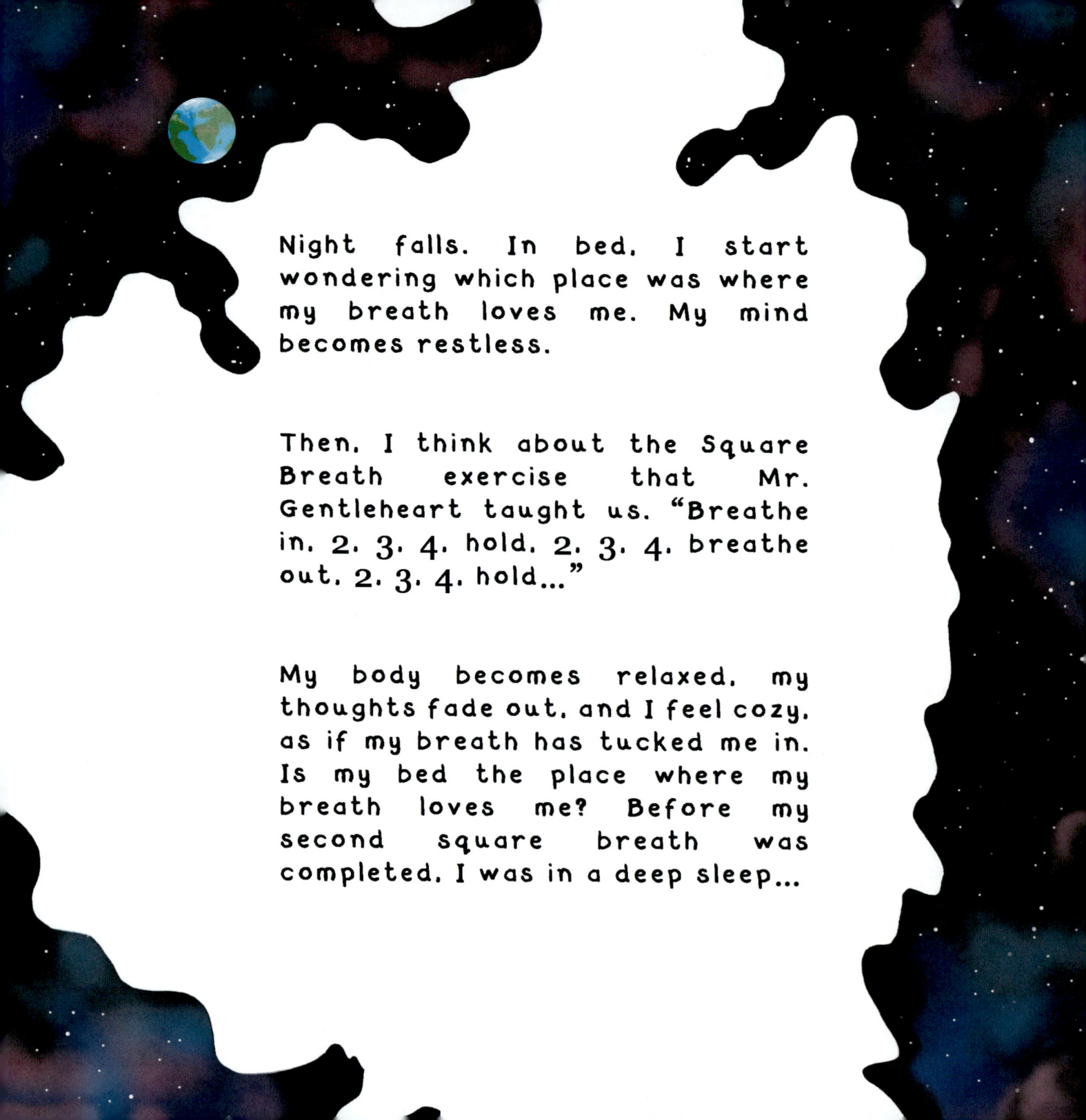

Night falls. In bed, I start wondering which place was where my breath loves me. My mind becomes restless.

Then, I think about the Square Breath exercise that Mr. Gentleheart taught us. "Breathe in, 2, 3, 4, hold, 2, 3, 4, breathe out, 2, 3, 4, hold…"

My body becomes relaxed, my thoughts fade out, and I feel cozy, as if my breath has tucked me in. Is my bed the place where my breath loves me? Before my second square breath was completed, I was in a deep sleep…

Mr. Gentleheart calmly says, "Slow down, April, and take a big breath."
And I do a very deep one with him. He asks me, "Why do you have to choose one place?"

This question, like a sign of spring, melts my wonders away. "Mr. Gentleheart, my breath loves me everywhere I go because my breath lives with me."

The breath is a gift given when we are born.
When we notice it and learn how to live with it,
We will feel full of gratitude.
Be curious and be friends with your breath.
Our lives are meant to be filled with peace and happiness.

ABOUT THE AUTHOR

Claire E. Hallinan, MAEd, was born in Japan and currently lives with her family in Washington. Claire has a passion for making sense of the world, building relationships, and inspiring people to find happiness in themselves. She is a writer, an entrepreneur, a Mindful Schools Certified Mindfulness Instructor, and a National Board Certified Teacher. Claire's books include her memoir, *Gift of Gratitude: Lessons from the Classroom*, and relationship-building book, *I Notice: Step-by-Step Guide to Transform Student Potential Through Building Intentional Relationships*. Claire also co-authored with her daughter *The Championslip: A Young Gymnast's Guide to Become a Fearless Champion on Her Own Terms*. Her first children's book, *My Breath Loves Me*, is an award-winning finalist in the Children's Mind/Body/Spirit category of the 2019 International Book Awards and has been translated in Japanese.

Connect with Claire:
claire.e.hallinan@gmail.com
https://claireehallinan.wordpress.com

Made in the USA
Coppell, TX
06 August 2021